D0535598

Creepy-Crawly Birthday

BUNNICULA
..and friends..

#6

Creepy-Crawly Birthday

by **James Howe**

illustrated by **Jeff Mack**

Atheneum Books for Young Readers
New York   London   Toronto   Sydney

Atheneum Books for Young Readers
An imprint of Simon & Schuster Children's Publishing Division
1230 Avenue of the Americas, New York, New York 10020
Text adapted by Heather Henson from *Creepy-Crawly Birthday* by James Howe
Book design by Michael McCartney
The text for this book is set in Century Old Style.
The illustrations for this book are rendered in acrylic.
Manufactured in the United States of America
First Edition
10 9 8 7 6 5 4 3 2 1
Library of Congress Cataloging-in-Publication Data
Howe, James, 1946–
Creepy-crawly birthday / James Howe ; illustrated by Jeff Mack.—1st ed.
p. cm. — (Bunnicula and friends ; #6)
Summary: When Toby Monroe has a birthday party, his pets' curiosity is aroused by seven strange suitcases, which they investigate, with surprising consequences.
ISBN-13: 978-0-689-85728-7
ISBN-10: 0-689-85728-4
[1. Birthdays—Fiction. 2. Animals—Fiction.] I. Mack, Jeff, ill. II. Title. III. Series: Howe, James, 1946– Bunnicula and friends ; #6.
PZ7.H83727Cr 2007
[E]—dc22
2006005028

To Garrett and Sela
—J. H.

For my brother Tim
—J. M.

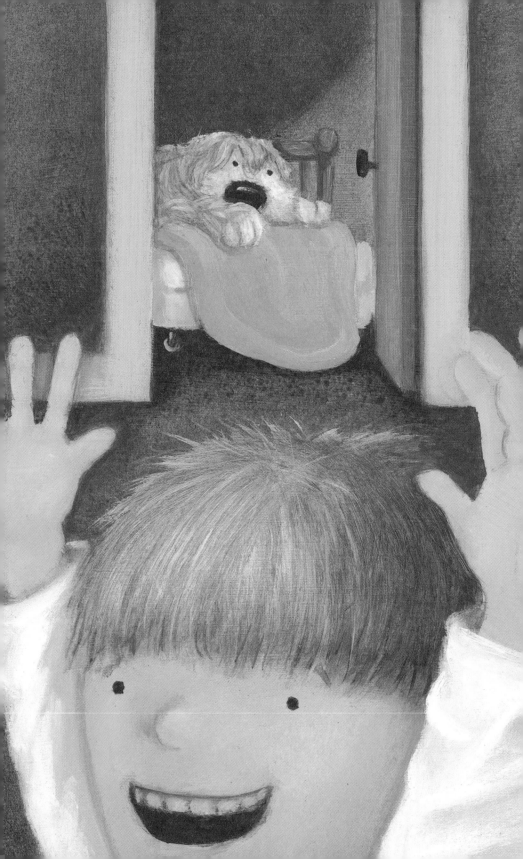

CHAPTER 1

Toby's Birthday

Toby's birthday was here at last.
I had been waiting for weeks.

I live with the Monroes. I like them all a lot, but Toby is my favorite. He lets me sleep on his bed, and he shares his snacks.

And he always has the best birthday parties.

"Remember last year?" I asked Chester and Howie.

"How could we forget?" Chester said dreamily.

"A whole gallon of ice cream!" Howie sighed.

We were all quiet, remembering and drooling.

Last year Mrs. Monroe had left the
ice cream out on the kitchen table.

"If we hadn't come along, that ice
cream would have melted!" Howie
said.

"There would have been a terrible
mess," Chester added.

We all glanced toward the kitchen
door.

3

"I guess it's too early for ice cream," I said.

"I guess so," said Chester.

So we went to join the party.

The living room was full of kids. Everybody was having a great time. There were balloons and fun games to play. Best of all, there were snacks.

We kept an eye on the messy kids. They were sure to drop tasty tidbits on the floor.

"Mrs. Monroe will be so happy!" Howie said. "She won't have to clean up after the party."

The thought of cleaning up reminded me of ice cream. I decided to head to the kitchen to see if it was time for dessert.

At the door, I heard voices.
I stopped to listen.

"I can't wait to show everyone my
special birthday present!" Toby was
saying.

"How about right before the cake?"
Mrs. Monroe asked.

"Great!" Toby said. "But remember,
Mom, it's a secret. I don't even want

Harold, Chester, and Howie to know. I want it to be a surprise."

"My lips are sealed," Mrs. Monroe said.

I rushed off before Toby and Mrs. Monroe came through the door and caught me listening.

A secret? Toby had never kept secrets from me before. He usually tells me everything. I wondered if the secret had anything to do with food.

Now I really wanted to find out what Toby's special birthday present was. And I knew just who would help me do it.

CHAPTER 2

Secrets and Surprises

Chester and Howie were all ears when I told them what I had heard.

"A surprise, eh?" Chester asked.

"I love surprises," Howie said.

"I don't," said Chester. He turned to stare at Bunnicula.

It was the middle of the day, so Bunnicula was sleeping inside his cage. That's what he does all day. He sleeps. He wakes up after dark.

"Toby didn't say anything about Bunnicula," I pointed out.

"But he did say something about a secret and a surprise," Chester replied.

"So?" I asked.

"So, we all know there have been a lot of secrets and surprises around here since Bunnicula came to live with us."

"Like vegetables and chocolate turning white?" Howie asked.

"Yes," said Chester.

"Like witches coming to visit and magicians pulling rabbits out of hats?" Howie asked.

"Exactly," answered Chester.

"Oh, brother." I sighed. Now I was sorry I had said a word to Chester about the secret surprise.

The thing is, Chester can get a little carried away sometimes. He actually believes that Bunnicula is a vampire bunny.

I can't really argue with Chester. Nobody can.

"That rabbit is mixed up in this somehow. I just know it," Chester said.

"Maybe we could check out Toby's presents—if we knew where Mrs. Monroe put them," I suggested.

Chester raised an eyebrow.
"*I* know where the presents are."

"What are we waiting for?" Howie
yipped. "Let's go!"

Chester led the way to Mr.
Monroe's study.

The room was filled with presents.

"How do we know which one is the special present?" I wondered.

"Well, there's only one way to find out," Chester said. "Use your sniffers."

Howie and I started sniffing through the presents.

"Nothing unusual here," I said.

"I haven't found anything either," said Howie.

Chester didn't say a word. He was staring into a dark corner. His tail was twitching.

"What are those?" he asked in a low voice.

I took a closer look.

"Suitcases," I said.

"Could that be Toby's present?" Howie asked.

"What would Toby want with seven suitcases?" I asked.

"I don't think those are normal suitcases," Chester said.

I groaned. Chester's imagination gets the better of him sometimes.

"Let me guess," I said. "They are really aliens in disguise, right? Suitcases from outer space?"

Then one of the suitcases started to move.

"The luggage is alive!" Howie yelped.

CHAPTER 3

Living Luggage

When I took a closer look I saw that there were holes in the suitcases. And there were eyes staring out of the holes.

"There are animals inside those cases," said Chester.

"Oh, no!" somebody cried. It was Toby's brother, Pete, coming into the study. Mrs. Monroe was right behind him.

"Sorry, guys, but you can't be in here," she said.

They grabbed us by the collars. The next thing we knew, we were in the cellar. And we were not alone.

Bunnicula was there with us.

"What's he doing here?" Howie asked.

Chester's eyes became little slits.

"Maybe he's here for the same reason we are. Think, Harold," Chester said.

"Do I have to?" I hated when Chester asked me to think.

"Toby didn't want us to know about his special birthday present," Chester explained. "Meanwhile, there are seven strange animals upstairs. And we're downstairs."

"So?" I asked.

"So, the Monroes are giving Toby seven new pets for his birthday!" Chester exclaimed.

"Why would they do that?" Howie whimpered. "Aren't we enough?"

Chester snorted. "Apparently not," he said. Then he added, "Well, I won't stand for it!"

"Me, either!" I said.

"Me, either!" said Howie.

"Follow me!" Chester ordered.

Luckily the cellar door wasn't locked, and there was no one in the kitchen.

We went quickly down the hall. The party was going full blast, so no one saw us. We stopped when we got to the door of the study.

"What's your plan, Chester?" I asked. Chester always has a plan.

"We're going to let them loose," Chester said.

"What?" Howie and I cried together.

"They're strange animals in a strange place," Chester explained. "Before you know it, they'll be running around, acting crazy. All we have to do is sit quietly and be perfect pets."

"That's not a bad plan," I said.

I pushed the door open and walked over to the suitcases. It wasn't hard to work the latches loose. Then I stood back and waited.

CHAPTER 4

Creepy-Crawlies

At first nothing happened. The suitcases were still.

I wondered if I had imagined them moving before. But there *was* a strange smell.

"Out, out!" I woofed.

One of the suitcases started to wiggle and shake.

And then another.

And another.

And out THEY came.

Howie went nuts right away.

I gave it a good six seconds before losing my cool.

"Let me out of here!" I yelled.

Chester and I got tangled up on our way out the door.

Howie got tangled up with the tablecloth in the dining room.

Toby's birthday cake went crashing to the floor.

Somebody started screaming.

"Snakes!"

"Rats!"

"Creepy-crawlies everywhere! What kind of party is this?"

Everybody rushed to the door, but
a strange man was blocking the way.
"My animals!" the man cried. "How
did they all get loose?"

"I'm sorry, Mr. Hu," said Mrs. Monroe. "We'll find them all, won't we boys and girls?"

The party turned into a search party.

I wanted to help, but Mrs. Monroe pushed us out the front door.

"You three have helped enough already," she said.

"So much for the perfect pet plan," I told Chester.

While we were sitting on the porch I noticed a van parked at the curb.

"Hu's Zoo," I read aloud.

"Who's who?" said Howie. "Well, I'm Howie and you're—"

I ignored Howie and went on reading. "Unusual Animals for All Occasions—Birthday Parties My Specialty."

I turned to Chester. "Nice going," I said.

Chester looked up at the sky. "It looks like it might rain," he said.

CHAPTER 5

The Real Surprise

After a while we sneaked back into the house to watch Mr. Hu's show. Mr. Hu was letting the kids gently pet the animals.

"See? The hedgehog rolls up into a little ball when you hold him," Mr. Hu explained.

"Wow! He feels like a hairbrush!" Toby cried.

"This is the weirdest birthday show I've ever seen," Chester muttered. "Whatever happened to clowns?"

Pretty soon Mr. Hu began to put his animals away.

One was missing.

"I'm sure it will turn up sooner or later," Mrs. Monroe said.

When Toby noticed us he gave us a pat.

"Sorry guys," he said. "I should have told you before. Mr. Hu has a rule. No pets in the same room as his animals."

Toby led us toward the back door. "Now I have a surprise for you."

I glanced at Chester. I wasn't sure how many surprises we could take in one day.

Toby opened the door. "It's a clubhouse!" he shouted. "Isn't it great?"

So this was Toby's special birthday present! A clubhouse with places for each of us. Toby was keeping it a secret because he wanted to surprise us.

"I can't believe we ever thought he would want any other pets!" I said.

"Yeah," said Howie. "Whose idea was that, anyway?"

Chester didn't answer. He was busy licking his tail. That's a cat's way of trying to act cool when he knows he's made a total fool of himself.

Back inside, we all sang "Happy Birthday" to Toby.

Mr. Hu had to go to another party. The Monroes promised to call him

as soon as they found his missing
animal.

"Maybe the little guy hid from
Mr. Hu on purpose," I said.

"Why would he do that?" Chester
asked.

"Well, it's so much fun here,
maybe he wanted to hang around,"
I answered.

Chester twitched his whiskers. "Really, Harold," he said, "that's the *battiest* thing I ever heard."